Sirena

A MERMAID LEGEND FROM GUAM

TANYA CHARGUALAF TAIMANGLO
ILLUSTRATED BY SONNY K. CHARGUALAF

Sirena

A MERMAID LEGEND FROM GUAM

by **Tanya Chargualaf Taimanglo**

Illustrated by **Sonny K. Chargualaf**

AuthorHouse™
1663 Liberty Drive
Bloomington, IN 47403
www.authorhouse.com
Phone: 833-262-8899

Because of the dynamic nature of the Internet, any web addresses or links contained in this book may have changed
since publication and may no longer be valid. The views expressed in this work are solely those of the author and do
not necessarily reflect the views of the publisher, and the publisher hereby disclaims any responsibility for them.

Any people depicted in stock imagery provided by Getty Images are models,
and such images are being used for illustrative purposes only.
Certain stock imagery © Getty Images.

Illustrated by Sonny K. Chargualaf

This book is printed on acid-free paper.

ISBN: 978-1-4520-5726-2 (sc)
ISBN: 978-1-4918-6793-8 (e)

Library of Congress Control Number: 2010910905

Print information available on the last page.

Published by AuthorHouse 03/15/2021

authorHOUSE®

Dedicated to OUR FATHER, Tedy Gamboa Chargualaf

The Guam sunrise peeked over the horizon,
warmth and brightness flooded Sirena's small room.
She awoke excited for another day of swimming.
She wondered how many chores Mama wanted her to do.

Breakfast was set and Mama was humming.
Sirena took her place at the table for two.
She asked out loud if her Godmother was coming,
but, Mama just rattled off a list of chores to do.

"Sirena, my girl, wash the clothes and get the coconut shells."

"Yes, Mama dear. I will do what I can do."

But, in Sirena's mind she was splashing in the water.

"That's not good enough, *neni,* get your chores done through and through!"

Mama called out to be back before noon,
as Sirena bolted to the river to rush through her chores.
"Come into the water," the river cooed, the river crooned.
Sirena obeyed, leaving the basket of clothes at the shore.

Time ticked away and Sirena swam and played.
The fiery sun hit the highest point in the hot Guam sky.
And Mama, at home knew her daughter had swayed
from her chores and what more she was swimming, undenied.

"Sirena! *Månu na gaige hao?*" Mama screamed out the door.
Godmother heard the anger and she changed her path,
For she knew Sirena was swimming and neglecting her chores,
Godmother feared Mama's anger and her wrath.

"That girl is swimming, I know she is!
She might as well change and become a fish!"

Godmother froze, hearing the worse
And did what she could to wage a countercurse.

"Please, stop my Sirena from transforming to a fish,
Keep her heart, which is mine, the way it always is."

Sirena dove deep into the cool river's blue,
A tingling and tickling swirled up from her feet.
She looked down at fins and wondered if it was true,
Scales sparkled and stopped where her heart and tummy meet.

Sirena felt both sad and happy for this wish.
She wanted to share this magic with her Mama but thought,
Would she still love me? Half girl and half fish?
And what if in Tun Pepi's net I am caught?

A feeling of freedom overtook the new mermaid.
Sirena longed to be in the deep azure ocean.
She turned back once to see two women who stayed,
At the shore—sad and crying with so much emotion.

Sirena waved one last wave then saw it returned.
She cried her last human tear and rose up in the air,
Diving into her new home, for a life she yearned,
Like foam in the sea, her old life now disappeared.

Mama swam everyday to be closer to her daughter,
Sirena, the beautiful girl cast away by a mother's ill wish.
Mama's tears dropped and flowed into the water,
Never to reach the child who had now become part fish.

It is said that Sirena can be seen by sailors,
And those who believe in great magic and myth.
It is said that Sirena can be caught with a net,
A net of human hair, but she is too crafty and too swift.

Tanya Chargualaf Taimanglo was born in 1974 to a Chamorro Army soldier and a South Korean beauty, Un Cha Kang. Her father is the late Siñot Tedy Gamboa Chargualaf. Tanya is the eldest child of three. Her brothers, Theo and Sonny K. Chargualaf reside on Guam with their families. Sonny collaborated with Tanya and created the stunning artwork of **Sirena: A Mermaid Legend from Guam**.

Tanya is the product of a Guam public school education. She graduated in 1992 from George Washington High School. She attended the University of Guam on a Merit Scholarship. She graduated with honors with a BA in English and Secondary Education in 1996. Tanya had an eight year career as an English and Creative Writing teacher at John F. Kennedy High School. Also, working proudly with the Tourism Academy. She taught alongside her late father, a Chamorro teacher and brother, Sonny--an art teacher. She has had work featured in Latte Magazine, University of Guam's Storyboard 6 and articles in local business magazines. She received the Who's Who Among America's Teachers award in 2000 and 2002.

Tanya married her childhood friend, Henry Taimanglo--a Navy Chief, in 2004 in the village of Asan. They currently reside in California with their two children. Tanya volunteers with the non-profit organization, CHE'LU, Inc. which strives to promote the Chamorro culture through education.